Little
HELPERS

michéle brummer everett

HOUGHTON MIFFLIN HARCOURT
Boston   New York

Hello, friend! Have you ever needed a helping hand? We all do from time to time, but some of us need the extra encouragement and love given by animal helpers. Instead of hands and feet like us, these animal helpers have paws, hooves, and soft fur, all of which make them very special.

CAT is a little helper in the hospital. She's an excellent snuggler, which makes people feel happy so they can get better soon.

HORSE is a little helper for those who have had bad things happen to them. Having Horse by their side makes it easier for people to talk about their problems.

LLAMA is a little helper in the children's hospital. Her cute outfits and soft fur put a smile on the kids' faces.

TORTOISE is a little helper on the airplane. He helps his owner to breathe deeply if flying feels scary.

SNAKE is a little helper for people who have seizures. She gives a gentle squeeze that means "Time to take some medicine!"

PIG is a little helper at the nursing home. Sometimes older people don't remember things. Pig helps them to smile and feel less confused.

MONKEY is a little helper at home. She can switch on the lights, open the fridge, and even scratch someone's face when they have an itch.

PARROT is a little helper for people who are upset or lonely.
She helps by saying things like "Take a deep breath now!"
and "You're the best of the best!"

FERRET is a little helper at school. Some kids feel like it's too difficult to speak to other people, and Ferret helps them be extra brave.

RABBIT is a little helper for those who are very old and very sick. Rabbit is almost like medicine, because she can make people feel better just by curling up on their laps.

DOG is a special helper for people who can't see or hear. He helps people to cross the road, get on the bus, and stay safe.

DOG's FRIEND is another little helper. If someone's blood sugar is low, this dog can smell it. "Thanks for the juice box, pup!"

These animals are all wonderful helpers! And even though we don't have paws, hooves, or soft fur, people can be just as helpful to each other. So keep an eye out for opportunities to be a little helper yourself to someone in need!

 CATS are great at providing comfort to people in hospitals. Studies have shown that simply petting a cat may lower blood pressure and boost immunity, making people get better faster.

 HORSES have unusually heightened senses that make them keenly aware of human emotions. The way they respond and interact with people can speed up the therapy process for those suffering from emotional disorders and traumatic experiences.

 LLAMAS are unusual therapy animals and help those who might be in physical or emotional pain. Llamas have soft fur and are especially social. The smiles and joy they bring to those in need is proven to reduce pain, depression, and fatigue, and to improve overall health.

 TORTOISES, along with other support animals, are allowed onto airplanes for free, as long as there is a note from the doctor. These animals provide comfort to people who might feel extreme fear or nervousness while in the air.

 SNAKES can warn about an oncoming seizure by giving a tight squeeze. They sense changes in blood pressure, which can indicate an oncoming episode. This gives their owners enough time to take medication or get to a safe place.

 PIGS have been used as therapy animals for those who have Alzheimer's disease. Their visits to nursing homes bring joy and reduce stress not only in patients, but family members and caregivers as well.

 MONKEYS are good helpers for people who are paralyzed. Nimble capuchin monkeys are particularly well suited for this work because they can be trained to learn important tasks such as opening bottles, adjusting eyeglasses, and reaching for things.

 PARROTS have the ability to imitate human speech and phrases. This enables them to be a calming influence on those who might be suffering from anxiety. Some have been trained to give words of encouragement during panic attacks. Parrots are fun and loyal companions but require a great deal of care. The work entailed promotes love and empathy and helps bond owner and pet.

 FERRETS are often used as companions for those with autism, especially children. They promote socialization, and studies have shown that autistic children are willing to be more communicative in the presence of an animal they have bonded with. Ferrets can be very playful and affectionate, making them a wonderful choice for children.

 RABBITS have the ability to be calm in new circumstances, which makes them perfect as therapy animals. They are especially good with the elderly, who might not be able to have pets of their own. The organization Bunnies in Baskets in Oregon allows people to book "bunny parties" that provide time with these highly socialized and affectionate rabbits.

 DOGS help their blind and deaf owners navigate the world and keep them safe. Such important work requires a lot of focus, so if you meet a Seeing Eye dog or hearing aid dog, it is best not to distract him. That means you shouldn't pet or interact with them when they're wearing their harness. If they're resting, you shouldn't pet or talk to them without their owners' permission.

 OTHER DOGS are trained to help diabetic owners manage their blood sugar levels. Dogs have an amazing sense of smell, and professional trainers are able to teach them how to distinguish between certain scents. If a human's blood sugar is too high the dog can sense a "fruity" aroma, whereas everyone has their own unique smell when their blood sugar gets low.

To Daniel and Simon

The images in this book were created using Adobe Illustrator
on a computer in an office looking out onto the Rocky Mountains.

The text type was set in Agenda.
The display type was handlettered by Michéle Brummer Everett.

Library of Congress Cataloging-in-Publication Data
Names: Everett, Michéle Brummer, author.
Title: Little helpers : animals on the job! / by Michéle Brummer Everett.
Description: Boston : Houghton Mifflin Harcourt, [2018]
Identifiers: LCCN 2017015652 | ISBN 9780544879553
Subjects: LCSH: Animals as aids for people with disabilities—Juvenile literature. |
Working animals—Juvenile literature. | Animals—Therapeutic use—Juvenile literature.
Classification: LCC HV1569.6 .E94 2018 | DDC 362.4/0483—dc23
LC record available at https://lccn.loc.gov/2017015652

Manufactured in China
SCP 10 9 8 7 6 5 4 3 2 1
4500694564